For yours, mine, and ours
—J.L.

For Haden, Chase, and Lily
—L.E.

For Theo
—A.E.M.

To Esther
—T.T.

Library of Congress Cataloging-in-Publication Data
Lynch, Jane, author.
Marlene, Marlene, Queen of Mean / by Jane Lynch, Lara Embry, and A. E. Mikesell ; illustrated by Tricia Tusa. — First edition.
p. cm.
Summary: "Marlene is the class bully until Big Freddy stands up to her." —Provided by publisher.
ISBN 978-0-385-37908-3 (trade) — ISBN 978-0-375-97329-1 (lib. bdg.) — ISBN 978-0-375-98232-3 (ebook)
[1. Stories in rhyme. 2. Bullying—Fiction.] I. Embry, Lara, author. II. Mikesell, A. E., author. III. Tusa, Tricia, illustrator. IV. Title.
PZ8.3.L9892Mar 2014 [E]—dc23 2013030729

MANUFACTURED IN CHINA
10 9 8 7 6 5 4 3 2 1
First Edition
Random House Children's Books supports the First Amendment and celebrates the right to read.

MARLENE, MARLENE, QUEEN OF MEAN

BY **JANE LYNCH**,
LARA EMBRY, PhD,
AND A. E. MIKESELL

ILLUSTRATED BY
TRICIA TUSA

Random House 🏠 New York

Let me
tell you
a story
of a girl
seeking glory,
who thought
that the
best thing
to do

was to pinch

and to kick
and to scowl
and to flick

and to block
children's way
to the loo.

Marlene, Marlene,
the queen of
the scene,
of the playground,

the sidewalk,

the school . . .

Marlene, Marlene,
the queen of the mean,
was known for being
quite cruel.

Though she
wasn't so tall
(not really at all),
the shadow
she cast was
IMMENSE.

She'd stand on a chair
to gloom and to glare,
making everyone
feel really tense.

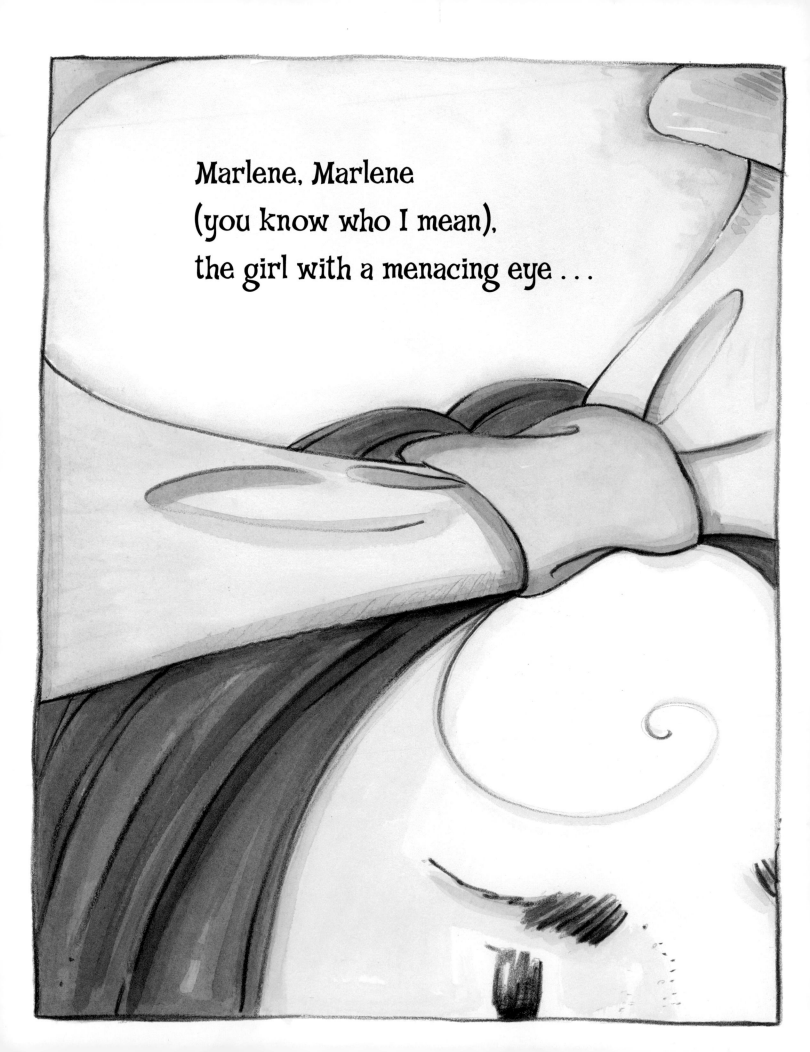

Marlene, Marlene
(you know who I mean),
the girl with a menacing eye . . .

her wrath cut
like daggers.
She'd strut and
she'd swagger,
till all the kids
started to—

"Why?"

asked Big Freddy,
his voice loud and steady,
being brave (and a little contrary).
"She's 'Mean Marlene,'
but really, I've seen,
she isn't so terribly scary.

"She's not very tall,
not really at all.
It's just her
shadow
that's
large.

"We cringe and we cower
and give her our power
because we all think
she's in charge!"

And with that, Mean Marlene
(who wasn't so keen
on her power beginning to fade)
put on her
best glower

and made her face sour—
but the kids were no longer afraid.

So Marlene
stiffened her back
and went on the attack,
unleashing her meanness
quite fully.

Though she kicked
and she pinched,
not a single kid flinched,
and Freddy said,
"You're just a bully."

After Freddy's decree,
they could see—could it be?—
that despite what she'd hoped to imply,

behind Marlene's glare,
no monster was there.
Mean Marlene was
starting to cry!

Her tears rose up to melt
all the anger she felt–

it flew

from her nose

in three sneezes.

Falling away like a cloak,
her meanness—it broke!
Into one hundred
twenty-three pieces!

Marlene, Marlene
had lost the routine
of her formerly
terrible self.

Since being a jerk
would no longer work,
she had to become
something else.

Her kindness
can slide
and her tone
can be snide
because
her change
is so recent.

(You see, it's a breeze
to learn how to tease;
it's harder, sometimes,
to be decent.)

And Marlene, at times,
commits (small)
friendship crimes
that her new self
might seem to forbid.

But she is,
more or less,
I'm sure
you can guess,
becoming a
much nicer kid.